Aliens Love Underpants

For Jason, my forever friend
– CF
For Anna, with all my love
– BC

First published in Great Britain in 2007 by Simon & Schuster UK Ltd

ISBN 978-0-545-33081-7

12 11 10 9 8 7 6 5 4 3 2 1   11 12 13 14 15 16/0

Printed in the U.S.A.   08

This edition first printing, January 2011

Book designed by Genevieve Webster

Aliens Love Underpants

Claire Freedman & Ben Cort

SCHOLASTIC INC.
New York Toronto London Auckland
Sydney Mexico City New Delhi Hong Kong

Aliens love underpants,
Of every shape and size.
But there are no underpants in **space**,
So here's a big surprise...

When aliens fly down to Earth,
They don't come to meet YOU...
They simply want your underpants—
I'll bet you never knew!

Their spaceship's radar bleeps and blinks
The moment that it sees
A fresh clothesline of underpants,
All flapping in the breeze.

They land in your backyard,
Though they haven't been invited.
"Oooooh, UNDERPANTS!" they chant,
And dance around, delighted.

They like them red, they like them green,
Or orange like wild pumas.
But best of all they love the sight,
Of Granny's spotted bloomers.

Mom's pink frilly panties
Are a perfect place to hide
And Grandpa's woolly long johns
Make a super-whizzy slide.

In daring competitions,
Held up by just one pin,
They dive into the long johns
To see how many can squeeze in!

They wear undies on their feet and heads,
And other silly places.
They fly undies from their spaceships and
Hold funny undies races!

As they go zinging through the air,
It really is pants-tastic.
What fun the aliens can have,
With underpants elastic!

It's not your neighbor's naughty dog,
Or his owner's funny game.
When underpants go missing,
The ALIENS are to blame!

But quick! Mom's coming out to fetch
The laundry in at last.
Wheee! Off the aliens all zoom,
They're used to leaving fast...

So when you put your underpants on,
Freshly washed and nice and clean,
Just check in case an alien
Still lurks inside, unseen!